Henry Waterfall

Rivelin Rhymes

Henry Waterfall

Rivelin Rhymes

ISBN/EAN: 9783337271527

Printed in Europe, USA, Canada, Australia, Japan

Cover: Foto ©Andreas Hilbeck / pixelio.de

More available books at **www.hansebooks.com**

VIEW OF THE VALLEY OF THE RIVELIN, FROM TOUGH WOOD.

Rivelin Rhymes.

HENRY WATERFALL.

"My father took me there;
For he his boyhood spent
In Rivelin Valley......"

SHEFFIELD:

J. ROBERTSHAW, PRINTER, ETC., ST. PETER'S CLOSE, HARTSHEAD.

1880.

The Rev. ALFRED GATTY, D.D.,

VICAR OF ECCLESFIELD,

SUB-DEAN OF YORK, &c.

REVEREND SIR,

I come to dedicate to you my book
of "Rivelin Rhymes," and hope it may be
worthy of your care. Your worth and wis-
dom, and your high and divine mission in
the service of the Christian Church, inspire
me with those respectful, obedient, and
trustful feelings with which I come.

You will not find in "Rivelin Rhymes"
that wonderful language, that intellect and
ever-increasing brightness of creative power
which the great poets have, who have made

the principal efforts of mankind their themes,
but the simpler effusions of one who has
spent many of his leisure hours in the delightful valley of the Rivelin, reading the
beautiful pages of Goldsmith, Burns, Words-
worth, and of our own James Montgomery
and Ebenezer Elliott.

In Rivelin, I "paddlet i' the burn, Frae
morning sun till dine;"—there, in hot
summer, the brooks "have little voice or
none;"—and where a homestead has once
been, "still many a garden flower grows
wild:"—and there, "Beneath the milk-
white thorn that scents the evening gale,"
I first read some of my verses (with critical
notices and good counsel to myself in a
magazine from your pen) to someone who
was with me. Your kindness has ever since
been cherished, if the good counsel has not
been quite followed. But I hope you will

spare my faults; and among my many roughnesses, I hope you will be able to perceive some traces of art; as when men find a slab or metal plate with design on, they rub it to see what it is.

I sincerely hope your days may be long yet, and that you will enjoy them with your usual health and cheerfulness.

Yours, with respectful obedience,

HENRY WATERFALL.

PREFACE.

It would have been better if my verses had been smoother, not so fragmentary, and more in accordance with the requirements of acknowledged poetry ; but I have not made much progress in the art; so, I must let them go as they are. In these days of book reading, it is perhaps, not quite as imperative that rhyme and measure should be so exact as when they had to assist memory in the days of tradition. But I must leave myself in the hands of my readers in this respect.

I publish my verses, because I think they express some of those feelings that affect the heart for good:—as when we gaze on the bold outlines of distant hills, mingling with clouds, we can fancy that there the souls of those we love and that love us, in changing shade and sunshine for ever dwell; or as when we hear the summer's breath sighing through the trembling grass on the edge of a precipice, we might fancy it to be a faint rustle of passing moments, or the leaves of a daughter's book that she lets slip whisperingly from her waxy fingers : or as when we reflect on the responsibility and dignity of finding ourselves in existence, and having a part to act ; when the world's trials do not appear so much like evils as exercises for those higher powers which God has given us. And by which exercises and His help, we may so gain in strength, that we may do much in the way of mastering the poverty, ignorance, and brutality which beset us, to smoothen down the asperities of our tempers, to keep watch over our hearts, and claim a victory.

I have gone after worldly pleasures, even when I have been conscious that I was departing from those virtues of pure, simple, and industrious life on which happiness depends. And that I might be at ease in the pursuit of these pleasures, I have sought them in common with inferior grades of men, and where it was not likely I should meet with reproof. I have slighted the opportunities I have had of promoting my social standing and spiritual welfare. I am soiled in the field of earth, and He whom I honour is far from me, and His face is turned the other way. Yet with none need this be so to the end of life; for although the past must for ever remain as we have left it, we may yet, in the days we have to come, merit the material blessings of well-spent time; and in our leisure hours and at home we may enjoy the charms of poetry (to which stock, O may I add a little!) and in the hour of death we may have the consolations of religion.

The composing of these rhymes has been a benefit to myself; it has led me to read more diligently our best authors; made me better acquainted with our language, and above all, convinced me that virtue and piety give the best charms to poetry, and the most lasting enjoyments to life.

CONTENTS.

PAGE.

Riuqlin Rhymes.

FLOWERS.

Man, spurn not flowers from the soil,
  But with thy fruits and herbs
Give them a place, where no turmoil
  Their paradise disturbs ;
For they were thy first playmates, meant
  To sanctify thy heart ;
For canst thou smell a flow'ret's scent,
  Nor sinful thoughts depart ?

WILD FLOWERS.

E'en early spring-time
Brings them forth, and then
   In any lowly nook,
Where poor thin soil is laid,
   You find them, if you look.

Like the children
Of a drunken father, that are
   Poor, sweet, and kindly spoken;
So long as grief has not
   Their mother's spirit broken.

How many fair
And lovely things the moulds
   Of earth send forth awhile;
And then they fade again
   To cold and clammy soil.

A child's first thoughts
Of heaven are best; it hopes
   To meet once more with those,
Who gathered with it here,
   The daisy and wild rose.

THE PRIMROSE.

Pale flow'ret of the field, beside
   The storm-torn hedgerows, thou
   Hast come forth, even now,
Ere blust'ring Winter's face is dried.

The clammy sod, that lies below
   The woodbine, is the bed
   Where thou hast raised thy head,
Wet with the showers of rain and snow.

Still as the spring-time hours advance,
   The sun comes out awhile,
   And then a brightened smile
Is on thy modest upward glance.

Anon the sky is dark with rain,
   And gusty showers rush
   Through ev'ry tree and bush,
And strike thy tender bloom again.

Though chilly be thy lot on earth,
   Sweet flower, a brighter day,
   I trust will yet repay,
The hardships of thy hapless birth.

And though we're here with sorrows laden,
   The weary soul must be
   Refreshed with joy, to see
In thee, a relic left of Eden.

THE DAISY.

Primroses, pinks,
Violets, and daffodils
   Have all the happy power
Of bringing pure days back ;
   So has this little flower.

Its field-wild scent,
And crimson edge, refresh
   Those memories of the past,
Which sweetest are through life,
   And dearest to the last.

And if the soul
Has dear remembrances
   Of earth in heaven, they 'll be,
Sweet flower, youth's happy days,
   And sinless things like thee,

Who seem'st to be
The very one, that made
   The first impression on
My boyish mind, and not
   A charm with time bygone.

FORGET-ME-NOT.

Alone, sweet flower,
There whiling away alone
  The sunny hour,
  It is thy lot
To bloom on life's wayside alone,
  Forget-me-not.

Mid herbage green,
Thy half-wild blooms alone,
  I might have seen,
  Or seen them not,
Blooming on life's wayside alone,
  Forget-me-not.

If not for me
Thy heavenly blue alone,
  Whose can they be,
  Or why? for what
Bloomest thou on life's wayside alone,
  Forget-me-not?

Is there an eye
That sees thee when alone?
In summer's sky,
That heeds thy lot,
Blooming on life's wayside alone,
Forget-me-not?

Some country child,
That's poorly clad alone,
Blue posies wild,
Of thine has got,
And says on life's wayside alone,
Forget-me-not.

The freckled face,
The sunburnt hands alone,
In many a place,
When days are hot,
Are seen on life's wayside alone,
Forget-me-not.

THE BRIER.

—

Where are those tender, silken roses gone,
  That late adorned thine arched, elastic
    stem;
Alas! they 've shed their petals one by one;
  Enamoured zephyrs have eloped with
    them.

With some eloped, with some a moment
    toyed,
  And left them shrinking, shrivelled on thy
    thorn,
Where thou beholdest them with charms
    destroyed,
  And seem'st to me in silent grief to mourn.

But do not let that grief become despair;
  Let faith outlive the day of transient pain;
For summer's glow shall winter's hurts re-
    pair,
  And thou in primal glory bloom again.

May even those that now are withered flowers,
  Fling perfumes forth to every passing wind;
As recollections of our happy hours
  Bring soothing sweets to cheer the troubled
    mind.

A SHOWERY MORNING IN SPRING.

How is the morning?
By the noise of the trees,
It rains—it rains!
And the flow'rets adorning
The grassy plains
And the leas,
Are nodding and dancing,
In the drops
That are glancing,
As glad as can be,
Rejoicing merrily—
And again and again,
The incessant rain
Pours!—it pours—
It roars—it roars—
It showers—it showers
On the new opened leaves, the grass and the
flowers.

The child stands
At the kitchen door;
And holds out its hands

To catch the drops
Of the rain that never stops ;
And again, and again,
The incessant rain
Pours—it pours—
It roars—it roars—
It showers—it showers
On the new opened leaves, the grass and the
flowers.

The housewife
Sets a tin,
To catch
From the thatch,
The rain therein ;
And as merry as life,
Like a kettle-drum it drums,
As fast as it comes ;
And again, and again
The incessant rain
Pours—it pours—
It roars—it roars—
It showers—it showers
On the new opened leaves, the grass, and the
flowers.

THE EDGE OF DARK IN WINTER.

How is the night?
By the lessening light
In the west,
Where the sun has gone to rest;
And by the wind that blows
Through the leafless hedgerows,
And that sighs,
As it tries
To get through the holes
Of the old stone walls,
It is frosty, and is likely to snow.

The hills are like giants of old,
Setting their backs up in the cold;
For they seem big and dark,
In their blankets of mist
Which they seem to twist
Round their feet,
And cover the dun hides
Of their dusky sides,
Where the dark folds meet:
And the sky is streaky and stark,
Where the evening star flickers like a spark.

The wintry wind roars,
Through the homestead sycamores,
Where the weather-vane squeaks,
And the old chimney reeks,
And the rapid streaks
Of the hurrying smoke
Curl and roke,
And are cast
Away on the furious blast ;
Like one out of her mind,
Who undresses
Her head, and throws her loose tresses
Away on the wind.

But though it is a moorland farm
The hearthstone is warm,
And the fire sheds a glare
On the happy faces there ;
And the old man in his chair,
Whose thin white hair
Has long been hoary,
Looks round upon all
With glances that fall
Like beams from the Land of Glory.

THE EMPTY HOUSE.

I looked in at the lone, empty house;
  I opened the squeaking, worn door;
I knew all the corners and nooks,
  And the dark, damp nicks of the floor.

The fire-grate was rusty and red,
  And cold were the cinder remains;
And the bars seemed to stare at the light,
  That came in through dim broken panes.

And the gaunt, bare walls of the place
  Re-echoed the sounds of my feet;
But were still as the grave when I listened;
  And my heart interruptedly beat.

I thought of the friends who had gone,
  As I gazed on those bars rusted red;
For they seemed like the skeleton ribs
  Of one I had known that was dead.

And wherever a fire has been made,
  In an old ruined castle or cot;
Or even where gipsies have been
  There's an interest that clings to the spot.

OLD WILLIAM'S FREEHOLD.

How changed! for I remember well
   The burning yule-log, the ale,
And the beef on the pantry bench,
   And old William's Christmas tale.

The mistletoe that hung upon
   An oak beam, the bright holly berry,
The mince pie, the red cheeked apple,
   And all that made yule-time merry.

When John used to play the hautboy,
   And James used to play the bass;
And smiling joy was depicted
   On white-haired old William's face.

And long ere daylight, old Betty
   Would bring out her Christmas cheer;
Ah! and as good a soul was she
   As ever brewed once a year.

What changes there are *in posse!*
   Since then the homestead has been sold,
And now it is pulled down,
   That once was William's freehold.

The old folks had long been dead
   The last time I went that road;
And John turned out rather drunken,
   And James and Rachel went abroad.

I've heard from James several times,
  And find he still keeps doing better;
He had just been elected a member
  Of Congress in his last letter.

He was never thought so sharp
  A lad as John; but he toiled,
And improved himself, while John
  Was the favourite and was spoiled.

But still John had some very good parts,
  And was far from being without worth;
In singing, his voice was one
  Of the few things that are on earth

Celestially beautiful.   He taught
  The scholars at Whitsuntide
Their singing; and he led the choir
  Of the Parish Church till he died.

And he was an honest man,
  The faithful trustee of many
Families; and none ever found
  That John was wrong a penny.

To Rachel, poor girl, but few
  Of this world's comforts were given;
She met with a worthless husband,
  But her hopes are fixed in heaven.

MAY MORN.

I.

At early dawn,
Among yon eastern skies
  The gray light softly breaks,
And from the cottage may
  Be seen the rosy cheeks

Of infant day,
While zephyrs cool and fresh
  Just move the ivy leaves,
And drops of moisture hang
  Along the old thatch eaves.

The little wren
Had sung its liquid song
  About the place, before
The iron latch did stir
  Which held the cottage door.

But now the fire
Is made of dry larch sticks,
  And cheerfully the kettle
Sings to the sun that shines
  Upon its brightened metal.

The merry clock
Strikes five that hangs against
  The yellow clay-washed wall;
And in the well outside
  Clear tinkling waters fall.

The cottager
Comes forth upon the lawn,
   And looks about ; but sight
At first can scarcely bear
   The floods of orient light,

Which glorify
The heavens, which make the earth
   Like Paradise, which raise
His thoughts to God, and fill
   His bounding heart with praise.

II.

Enjoyment is
Expressed in happy looks
   And voice on all sides round,
By soaring larks above
   And insects on the ground ;

By new leaves on
The trees that seem to feel
   The pleasures of the morn ;
By May-flowers in the brake,
   And blossoms on the thorn.

The thrush in flute
Notes, mellow, mixed with shrill,
   Wild variations, utters
To his mate melting love,
   Whose joyous plumage flutters.

The hare, the ox,
The horse, the lamb alike
 On heaven's broad bounty feed;
And sweets of life enjoy
 Upon the dewy mead.

III.

And pleasant sounds
Of water running o'er
 Yon distant mill dam's weir,
In many a swell and cadence
 Come in the placid air.

IV.

How pleasant is
The early morning's breath
 Among these groves and alleys!
How joyous are the birds
 Whose music fills the valleys!

The skies are clear;
For not a cloud is seen
 In all the deep blue West,
Nor in the East, save jewels
 Upon Aurora's breast.

The sandstone rocks
Form many a precipice,
 On which the sunlight shines,
That gilds with aerial gold
 Its craggy creviced lines.

But in the dells,
The pine plantations
   Intercept the sunlight's rise;
Where many a massy,
   Moss-encumbered fragment lies.

While on the hills,
Uprising strata lift
   Their great crags in the air;
Where many a fancied form
   Their storm-worn outlines bear—

The Toad's Mouth, Lot's
Wife, and the Giant's Head
   Still keep their dizzy height,
Amid the etherial blue,
   And morning's rosy light.

v.

Bright mountain-land,
In this chaste hour, when
   Dissipation lies asleep,
The hearty tourist wakes,
   And climbs the rocky steep,

To see the sun
Rise, whose refulgent beams,
   In brightening colours, dye
The reddened mountains, and
   The roseate-tinted sky.

He sees how broad
The stretching landscape is !
    How wide the vales! how grand
The mighty forms of earth,
    And feels his soul expand !

He cannot
Contemplate such scenes, nor breathe
    An atmosphere so pure,
And still his chastened mind
    Its baser thoughts endure.

To converse with
The beautiful, the pure,
    The boundless, must remove
The bondage of the heart,
    And make more space for love.

VI.

Beside the old
Rude turnstile, where the
    Footpath enters in the shade,
Two youthful lovers meet,
    By promise last eve made.

For then the day
In carmine grandeur set,
    When walking they presaged
A charming sunrise, and
    To meet this morn engaged.

So now they
Promenade the lawn ; and their
　Chaste conversation tells,
How love's enraptured hour
　All pleasure else excels.

For heartfelt bliss
Each lover's beating bosom
　Fills ; how could it miss,
When Youth and Beauty meet
　On such a morn as this ?

With them it is
The very spring-time of
　Their lives, the happiest day
They 'll have on earth, the
　Brightest of their brightest May.

They have no thought
Of sorrow coming fast
　To blight each loving heart,
As years of youth—nay e'en
　As hours of morn depart !

'T is well they think
Not thus, for now their minds
　Are happy, clinging fast
To scenes their memories
　Shall cherish to the last

Of this world's life,
When they in wedlock may
   Have lived through years of pain ;
Or may this morn have parted
   And never met again.

VII.

My own dear one,
Don't we remember well
   The pleasant walks we went
Among your father's fields,
   When our gay spirits lent

Ideal charms
To those delightful scenes,
   And to those bright past hours;
Since which we have not seen
   Such May-time or such bowers?

The very
Heart-aches that we suffered then,
   Fond memory keeps in store ;
And if they 've left a pain,
   'T is that they 'll come no more.

VIII.

A few short years
Ago, and you were then
   A witty, wayward girl,
Who prized a lover's heart
   As it had been a pearl,

To wear sometimes
And then to leave aside ;
   And if he e'er complained,
Coquettish answers or
   Disdainful looks obtained.

But all things yield
To love ; and in my house
   You 're now as good a wife
As e'er to husband's weal
   Devoted wifehood's life.

Frugality
Like yours, no baser bond
   Than marriage can secure ;
And without Heaven's regard,
   No motives are so pure.

Your old folks now
Are dead, and all your youth's
   Mates scattered far away
'Mong new connections that
   Engage their thoughts : they may

Sometimes think of
You, when Reflection's hour,
   From daily toils apart,
Finds time to look among
   The keepsakes of the heart.

These little ones
Now hold you here, in chains
   Made of the wild flower's stem ;
And Love must fold his wings
   To stay awhile with them.

And oh, may grief
Ne'er hurt your tender breast,
　　Whose worst sin, is that mild
Fond selfishness, a mother
　　Owns towards her child!

From earthly dregs
Like these, God's help alone
　　Can make love's chalice free,
And purify it, fit
　　For immortality.

From rank to rank
In love the prayerful heart
　　Succeeds, still gaining strength
To make those sacrifices
　　Which prepare, at length,

Our being to work
With God, in labours which
　　Shall heal the wounds of strife,
And which shall be the sweets
　　Of higher heavenly life;

We shall not
Slumber, rapt in dreams of bliss,
　　Nor be annihilated,
But living, loving still
　　From earth's clay elevated.

CHRISTMAS-MORN.

I.

Hark ! hark ! melodious strains of music
    break,—
'Tis morn of Christmas-day !
The folk at yonder mansion wake ;
    For there the minstrels play.

The old moon shines o'er snow-clad plains,
    And in the cottage peeps ;
While listening to the distant strains
    The swain no longer sleeps ;

But rises from untroubled rest,
    To raise the window sash,
And hear them play, while on his breast,
    The morning air blows fresh.

The cold breeze moves the home-spun
    sheet,
    And makes the curtains tremble ;
It brings harmoniously sweet
    Tones heavenly sounds resemble.

And then his little Annie wakes,
    Who lifting up her head,
Exclaims " Father," and him she seeks,
    But finds him not in bed.

" Whist ! love, whist ! father is there,
    Beside the window sill,
The music from afar to hear
    Then rest love and be still."

So kindly does the mother speak
    Unto her darling child,
And when 't has fondled her warm cheek,
    Again 't is reconciled.

And then a moment all is still,
    And then the low winds play,
And then they hear the music swell,
    And then it dies away.

But yet melodious sounds the breeze,
    As if it voices bore ;
At last they say—'t is but the trees,
    And music must be o'er.

Then on the glowing orbs of night
    The father turns his eyes,
And on the mountains robed in white
    Where snow unbounded lies.

To them the glad time does impart
    A taste of heavenly bliss ;
For music lingers in the heart
    Where happy virtue is.

II.

" O look !" cries Annie, pointing far ;
  " Before you leave the window—
O, father look ! that pretty star
  That twinkles over yonder.

" Do you not see it ?—O mother see !
  'Tis through that other pane !
Its glittering light comes straight to me ;
  I see it, oh! so plain !

" With one side green, the other red ;
  It seems as though it rolled ;
O father, lift me out of bed ;
  I care not for the cold."

" My dear child," both parents say,
  " It is so keen and raw,"—
But Annie cries—" A moment, pray
  O, mother let me go !"

" Well, well," the father makes reply,
  " She shall the snowy plain
Behold, the moon and starry sky,
  And then she 'll sleep again."

He takes her from her mother's side,
  And haps her in her night-dress,
To see the moon-lit world so wide,
  Laid in its wintry white-dress.

The Polar Star is shining north,
　And Sirius rolling clear,
The waning moon bright o'er the earth,
　And all the world is fair.

The frozen river's silvery breast
　Reflects the lunar ray ;
And all is quietness and rest,
　Save minstrels on their way.

Then on the glowing orbs of night
　They turn their wondering eyes,
And on the mountains robed in white
　Where snow unbounded lies.

LITTLE ANNIE'S LAMENTATION.

'T was afternoon,
  The day was hot,
No zephyr waved the corn, 't was sultry,
  Close in every spot.

The sky was cloudless,
  The June sun shone,
When Annie went to get wild roses,
  In the old grass lane alone.

Among the briers,
  Where roses grew,
Little Annie sang to herself, like bees
  That o'er the roses flew.

With a flowery wreath,
  Her white straw hat,
Little Annie trimmed, as by the harebells,
  And in the shade she sat.

Above an hour,
  That summer day,
Little Annie sang and played by herself,
  And her song then died away.

She seemed thoughtful,
  And she sighed with heat;
Little Annie cared no more for roses,
  The roses smelling sweet.

And at her side,
    Her hat was laid;
She heeded no more that flowery hat,
    And little Annie said:

" Emily's dead,
    Away she's carried;
She'll come to play with Annie no more,
    She never will,—she's buried.

And Leila too
    Lives a long way—
Far o'er yon distant sunny hills;
    She'll never come to play.

And Mary Wood
    Has long since gone;
And Annie is left to play with flowers,
    The summer day alone."

The bees still murmuring,
    In roses crept,
They laboured on with summer noise,
    And little Annie wept.

LEILA.

"I see not sister Leila—
　Mother, she is not here;
I see you all but Leila—
　Mother, she is not here."

"Alas! thy sister Leila—
　Once innocent and fair,
No more is sister Leila—
　She lives—we know not where.

We never hear of Leila—
　For ever she is fled;
Thou ne'er must look at Leila—
　We would that she were dead."

"I will see sister Leila—
　Though lost to you and truth;
I 'll seek for sister Leila—
　Once innocent in youth."

"To see thy sister Leila—
　'T will mar for evermore
That brighter thought of Leila,
　Thy memory ever bore."

"I see not sister Leila—
　Mother, she is not here;
I see you all but Leila—
　Mother, she is not here."

THE LOVER'S LEAP.

The North-East wind was cold;
   The day was drear to dree;
On the sea the white waves rolled,
   And the beach was solitary.

The gale was strong and breme,
   And heaving was the sea;
And the white-winged seabird's scream,
   Was a scream so solitary!

When on a cliff so bare,
   Where shrubs could never be,
Stood a maid with long loose hair,
   And that maid was solitary.

Awhile she stood and gazed,
   Then bent upon her knee,
And to heaven her locked hands raised,
   And that prayer was solitary.

The rock on which she knelt,
   Was beetling o'er the sea,
Where the gull its nest had built,
   And that place was solitary.

She cried in bitter anguish—
　　The brink was o'er the sea,
Where she screamed—"Why, why languish,"
　　And that scream was solitary.

She stretched her arms above,
　　As she from earth would flee;
And she leaped—for despised love
　　Had made that maid so solitary.

She fell into the wave,
　　When none were there to see;
And it soon closed o'er her grave,
　　And that grave is solitary.

It might have never been;
　　For yet the heavy sea
Breaks its waves in white and green,
　　On that rock so solitary.

All human hopes and fears
　　As nothing seem to be—
And the elements and years
　　Work out earth's destiny.

A DIRGE.

———

Not a stirring leaf was seen,
Deathly still was every tree,
And they looked a lighter green,
When the day was dark and gloomy.

Not a tulip moved its head,
All was calm as it could be ;
Peonies were brighter red,
When the day was dark and gloomy.

Black and low and near the ground,
Seemed the awful clouds to be ;
With a light horizon round,
When the day was dark and gloomy.

Like a mirror was the lake ;
In its water I could see,
Light green trees and verdant brake,
When the day was dark and gloomy.

All at once, when not a breeze
Waved a reed upon the lea,
Crash ! a whirlwind smote the trees,
And the day was dark and gloomy.

And I heard a funeral dirge,
In a mournful minor key,
Reach me from the grave's clay verge,
When the day was dark and gloomy.

And it solemnized my soul,
Poring on eternity ;
When the thunder 'gan to roll,
And the day was dark and gloomy.

A PRAYER.

God of man, to Thee I pray—
  Save me from mine enemy ;
Give me now that special good
  Thy goodness has in store for me.

Lift me from this darkening pit
  Of rapine, violence, woe, and death ;
Let me come to happier climes
  Of peace and love and lighter breath.

Let me live among the just,
  With the merciful and kind ;
Let me join my friends again ;
  Leave me not so far behind.

Cheer my sinking, painful heart ;
  Aid me, help me with Thy grace,
That I may raise my bended form,
  To see displeasure leave Thy face.

HIGH NOON IN SUMMER.

I.

At noontide, when
The summer's burning sun
Seems nearer to the eye
That is half shut, the hills
In composed grandeur lie,

Like sphinxes gazing
With their gray worn faces
At the high noon sun,
As they have ever since
Upheaving periods done.

So mute is all
The landscape round, that e'en
The solitary fir trees cease
To sigh, and all things else
Are hushed in slumberous ease.

Among the cliffs
The stillness is as still
As death, and in the heat
Of such high noon as this
You hear your own heart beat.

The wild heath smells,
Too luscious for the brain,
The mouse-ear hawk-weeds blaze
Their yellow in the eye
That fain would shun their gaze.

II.

I recollect
Once labouring in a hot,
Dry sandstone quarry, where
The sun's reflected rays
Were more than I could bear.

And, weary of
The burning gravel, I
In some low cabin gat,
That smelt of peat; and all
The afternoon, I sat

In thought of
Sunny, sandy lands, where goss
And wild sage flowers grew;
And every now and then
The work bees by me flew.

But whence they came,
Or whither went, I knew
No more, than thro' the sky,
They with a dree hum went
On express business by.

While zephyr bees
Reposing in the air,
On wings invisible, spent
Their dreamy, careless lives
Among the wild thyme's scent;

And stone-chats flit
About the hot, unsheltered,
Barren, rocky places,
Chattering like glass
Beads shook in pencil cases.

III.

And then I looked
Out far from that hill side,
On many distant miles
Of world-sized landscape round,
In plains and mountain piles,

Where wandering, wild
Imagination still
Might range without a fetter,
And unencumbered with
A pencil, pen or letter,

Among the scenes
That change with melancholy,
Chance love, despair or hope,
As bits of stained glass change
In a kaleidoscope.

IV.

And then I thought
  Of mankind as a whole,
And individually,
  That out of all that are
That one could but be me :

  That consciousness
  Revives again, and I
Again shall live, a breath
  Upon the earth, between
The jaws of Birth and Death.

  I looked at Death,
  Not without fear, shrank from
The thought that I should solve
  Into the mass again,
And never more evolve

  To individual
  Life, and on the other
Hand, I dared not think
  Of passing as I was
Beyond this mortal brink.

V.

And then a thought
   Came to my aid and said—
" Pass through a land like this,
   And thou shalt come to higher
Spheres of happiness.

  " Then master now
   Thyself ; for thou canst not
Dwell on the mountain range,
   Sole spirit of the waste ;
And noting every change

  " That frets with time
   Through this chaotic world,
From present to the past ;
   Nor watch a crumbling rock
While ever it will last.

VI.

  " Thou mayest do much
   With thinking, and thou wilt ;
But everlasting breath
   Thou 'lt never reach, but by
The simpler way of faith.

  " Yet contemplation
   Of such mighty scenes,
Will certainly improve
   The mind ; but 't is thy nature's
Better part to love.

" And Love a kindly
   Intercourse desires,
Or what on earth could save
   Thee from that coldness which
Is human nature's grave?

" Then make thyself
   Acceptable to them
On whom thy joys depend ;
   For dear relationships
Will never, never end.

" Improve thyself
   That edifying may
Be what thou would'st express,
   Describing still the way
Through earth to happiness."

THE SETTING SUN.

Setting was the expanded sun,
Dipping slowly in the ocean;
   Glittering was the briny main,
Like a minster's western window
   Shining on a distant plain.

Stretched and few were remnant clouds
O'er the half-quenched orb of day,
   Mottled, flaky, silvery, bright,
Like the golden forms of fishes
   Basking in the streams of light.

All was silent on the beach,
Save the lisping, tiny wave,
   When the sun's last lingering glance
Waning, lessening, died away,
   Mid the water's wide expanse.

Then I thought that he had gone,
Like a friend who leaves behind
   Him a parting halo of
Happy recollections, bright
   With the golden charms of love.

CROOKES VILLAGE.

A MORNING WALK IN RIVELIN.

"O Life! how pleasant in thy morning,
   Young Fancy's rays the hills adorning."
                                        BURNS.

'T was Sabbath morning ;
No breeze had then awoke
   When I made an early sally,
To hear the birds carol
   Whose music filled the valley.

The sun had risen ;
'T was nearly four o'clock ;
   And his shining I could trace
On hillocks in the fields,
   By many a swampy place.

The West was clear,
Where distant hills arose
   With rocky summits high,
Piercing the azure blue
   Of that beautiful western sky.

The mill was silent ;
The water-wheel was standing ;
   Yet through the sluice could steal
Small squirting streams of water,
   Which rained within the wheel.

The clear water
That babbled in the by-dike
  Alternate stood in pools;
For the stream was low, and the trout
  Were darting from their holes.

The stone-chats flew
About the massive rocks,
  Which like to tablets were;
And the stroller his luncheon
  Had often eaten there.

As I was walking
A something o'er the wall
  I heard, that made me stay,
And looking 't was a horse
  Which startled plunged away:

He galloped off,
And his clumsy ironed hoof
  Struck heavily the ground;
But ere he 'd galloped far,
  He stayed and looked around.

So I was walking
Enjoying as I went
  The calmness of the scene,
The singing of the birds,
  And the trees that looked so green.

Till in the West
The hills were looking duller,
  And thickening to a mist,
A cap upon their heads
  Descended white and fast.

And lowering yet
The mighty volumes white,
  The thick and chilly damps,
From the summits of the hills
  Were creeping down the swamps;

And soon the sky
Was clouded every way;
  The sun no longer shone,
The hills were all obscured,
  And the valley seemed alone.

And even to the mill
The lowering mist came down,
  Condensing on the trees,
Which soon were dripping wet;
  And the leaves showed not a breeze.

Beside a wall,
The fence of pastured ground,
  A heifer lonely stood,
And her heavy breath was smoking,
  As she quietly chewed her cud.

The rising steep
Through the mist was dimly seen,
  And hay-cocks which were there
Were small and far between,
  For the land was steep and bare.

Not very far
Nor very many hay-cocks
  Could I see up the steep,
For o'er the hillocky fields
  The mist did slowly creep.

The wild briers
Among the zig-zag hedges
  That straggled up the hills
Were weeping in the mist
  O'er little tinkling rills.

I saw a brier
With its branches hanging o'er
  A gray, old sandstone wall ;
And there I pulled a rose
  Which made the drippings fall.

I got another
From a low and bushy brier
  That a whiter petal bore,
And its scent was different
  From that I pulled before.

The verdant brake,
The glassy mill-dam's margin
  In the water its shadow threw,
And swallows under that brake
  Touched the water as they flew.

The thickening mist
Began to be a Scotch
  One, turning into rain
Which drove me home, resolved
  To come some morn again.

With morning sunshine,
With light and happy feet
  I began my early sally,
A mist came o'er my prospect,
  And wept through all the valley.

COLD WELL.

My way was long,
The hill was steep,
And on the short, smooth, trodden grass
My feet were hard to keep.

While in the sun
The hawk-weeds grew,
And on the ragworts wild bees slept,
And swarms of insects flew.

That hilly field
The cows had bared,
For scarcely anything but harebells
And buttercups was spared.

And toiling there
I often stayed
To look upon the woods which at
The mountain's feet were laid.

It is a grand,
Delightful scene,
To view that space of trees : when all
Their tops of varied green,

In mingled shades
Of light, you catch,
It nought but sea, or wilderness,
Or fairy land could match.

But soon enjoyment's
Power was spent ;
And pleasureless became the hayfield's
Smell and wild-rose scent.

Still up the steep,
With languid feet,
I toiled, and scarcely knew what ailed
My limbs, oppressed with heat,

Until I found
A stone trough, filled
With water clear and cold as e'er
From veins of hillside rilled,

Where, spreading wide,
A hawthorn grew :
That was an old and bushy tree,
And there its shadow threw.

That pleasant well
I passed not by,
But stayed to see its glassy surface
Bear the water-fly :

To see the mossy
Fountain wimple
From its dark recess, and in
The rosy daylight dimple ;

Then, like a silver
Sceptre, drop
Into the basin, making beads
That ran along the top

Of that bright mirror
To its edge,
In which there was an outlet, like
A hole made for a wedge.

And in the bottom,
All the bright
Sand seemed obliquely moved by pure
Refracted rays of light.

And I saw in
It, as I drank,
The harebell's bloom reflected there,
That grew upon the bank.

Then to that little
Limpid pool
A milkmaid came, and she was bearing
A milkpail and a stool.

A clean, white hood
Was on her head ;
Her dairy-gown was spotted blue ;
Her dairy-skirt was red.

That sandstone trough,
Though hard, was worn
Quite hollow on the side which oft
That milking pail had borne.

As in the water
Her pail found rest,
Put there to cool the milk within,
The maiden I addressed.

" What famous rill
Is this, please tell;
It perhaps has medical use, or may
Be called St. Anthony's Well?"

As in her hand
Hung by her side
Carelessly her three-legged milking stool,
The maiden thus replied—

" This icy stream
Is called ' Cold Well,'
And children's whooping cough within
The sound of our Church-bell

Is cured by it,
Or by a ride
Upon the bear-ward's bear for pence,*
Which comes at Whitsuntide.

---

* It is an old superstition to put children on the
bear's back to cure whooping cough. Sometimes a bit
of the bear's hair would be cut off for the child to wear
on its breast.

Besides being here
And full the same
It ne'er denied a stranger drink
　　Whoever thirsty came ;

But ever flowed
Beneath this tree
With no remembrance of a change
　　In the oldest memory."

And when she 'd gone
I watched that stream,
Still bubbling in the mossy trough,
　　Till rapt as in a dream ;

And saw it bring
Small grains of grit
With it, and wasting still the hill
　　Away, bit after bit,

As tho' it were
An hour glass
To run while e'er the world's years of
　　The human period pass.

THE BRACKEN FIRE.

I.

The day was clear,
  'T was calm and still ;
I only heard the dead leaves fall,
  And wayside babbling rill.

I saw a cot
  Among the trees
That skirt the woodland lane that
  Stranger's eye scarce ever sees.

The door was fast,
  And through a pane
I looked, but all was still ; they 'd gone
  Somewhere along the lane.

A black cat stared,
  The sneck was out,
Nor did she tell me where it was
  Though hid somewhere about.

I saw the house-leek
  On the eaves,
The flower pots, and besom reared
  Beside a heap of leaves.

That day they 'd left
  Their fastened door,
Near which a robin whistled long,
  Perched on a tub turned o'er.

I stood and listened ;
   No foot I heard,
For nothing moved but falling leaves,
   And robin, a lonely bird.

He hopped about
   The dark green holly,
And sang that low, sweet, Autumn song
   That 's touched with melancholy.

I came away,
   Oft looking back,
For still I thought I heard a foot,
   That followed on my track.

II.

Then on the lane
   I wend my way,
And ne'er enjoyed a ramble more
   Than on that autumn day.

I strayed among
   The bramble waste,
And ate a berry which frost had given
   An insipid taste.

The hips were bright
   Upon the brier and red,
And on the twigs the hedge sparrow
   Its plaintive ditty said.

III.

But when the sun
　Was getting low,
As day advanced I saw a smoke
　Rise from the vale below ;

And presently
　I saw the place
Whence came that blue ascending streak
　I in the sky could trace.

A woman who
　Was near the spot
Was cutting withered bracken with
　A sickle that she 'd got.

And when upon
　The fire she threw
Her handfuls fresh, the smoke
　Ascended light, and blue.

She left it and then
　Again returning
With bracken in her sunburnt hand
　She kept the fire burning.

And though the sun
　Was very bright
It struggled with the hissing stalks
　And sun's more powerful light.

The sunshine made
   The forky flame
Look pale and thin, and light the fumes
   That from the bracken came.

And as the smoke
   Rose high and higher
She put her handfuls on the flame
   And wandered round the fire.

IV.

I wondered why
   That fire she kindled,
And why she fed it still with bracken
   Which still to ashes dwindled.

I asked her why
   That fire she made,
And why she kept it burning thus
   And this the woman said—

" I 'm burning brake
   To make potash ;
It does instead of soda, and
   I use it when I wash.

" To-day, I thought
   I 'd leave my cot,
And burn as many ashes as
   Would fill this earthen pot."

v.

There seemed to me
  To be a rhyme
And lesson in that fire, I could
  Not help but think, that time

Burnt out the same;
  And as we spend
Its years, so shall be what is left,
  When life comes to an end.

And as that jar
  Was filled that day
Would be the measure of the soul
  When life had died away;

And as I mused
  She damped the fire
And put its ashes in the dark,
  Brown urn of clay, stood by her.

She wanted them
  For use, and who
Shall say the ashes of our years
  Shall not be wanted too?

THE THRUSH.

Cold wintry clouds have veiled the sky
  The whole March day, sweet bird;
And e'en when storms have driven by,
  Thy wild love song we 've heard.

Thou knowest well Spring time is near;
  And tho' a wintry day
Doth intervene, thou hast no fear,
  But sing'st its hours away.

But now inclement eve descends,
  The winds are whistling strong,
And ere the stormy darkness ends,
  What gusts may sweep along.

When showers of hail, in furious flight,
  Drive on the piercing wind;
When howls the tempest in the night,
  What refuge dost thou find?

Some sturdy holly's scanty shelter,
  That rattles in the storm,
Is all that bears the furious pelter,
  And shields thy tender form.

Still safe—for not that holly yet
　　Shall from its place be torn ;
'T were folly, death, perchance, to flit ;
　　Then rest thee, bird, till morn.

And then, perhaps, the final night
　　Of Winter may have passed ;
And have arrived with morning's light
　　Congenial Spring at last.

THE TITLARK.

The morning was dull,
    In the night we 'd had rain,
And the trees were all still,
    As they hung o'er the lane.

The wheat stalks were swelling,
    The hawthorns were weeping,
The sweetbriers smelling,
    The hawkweeds were sleeping;

The church bell was ringing,
    So clearly, so plain,
And the titlark was singing;
    That morn we 'd had rain.

The briers were wet,
    Leaves, flowers, and all,
Where the titlark had lit,
    On an old sandstone wall.

The brambles there grown,
    Were all dripping with rain,
Whence the lark had soon flown,
    To sing down again.

Thus times without end,
   He was rising to sing ;
So contented to spend
   All the days of the Spring.

His small cup of pleasure
   Was full to the brim ;
And though scanty its measure
   'T was plenty for him.

THE BLACKCAP WARBLER.

He 's here!—be still! I 've waited long,
   Thou pretty warbler, laid
   In silence in this shade,
That I may hear thy sylvan song.

O how untame that glance of thine
   Is, as thou tak'st each hop,
   Towards the very top
Twig, where the honeysuckles twine!

Where but a leaf thou seem'st, among
   Those growing on that spray;
   For thou art light as they;
And zephyrs waft thee all day long.

Thy ditty is at first so low
   And soft, that I laid here,
   Who seldom get so near,
When it commences scarcely know.

It swells with joy; and O how fine
   The rapid runs and trills;
   And every change that fills
That sweet, untutored song of thine!

And while those liquid warblings last,
   That upstretched throbbing throat
   Pours out the wildest note
That ever charms the woodland waste.

THE ROBIN.

The wind in the key-hole was mourning,
  We had finished our evening repast ;
When the fire was cheerfully burning,
  And the night was enclosing us fast.

The snow had continued all day ;
  And filled every crevice and rift ;
And the eastern blast blew it like spray
  Into many a beautiful drift.

I saw in the tempest that night,
  As it howled o'er the wintry waste,
On a twig in the dreary twilight,
  Was perched poor Robin Redbreast.

He hopped on the low garden-wall,
  Where often we saw that the haze
Of dull winter light at nightfall,
  Reflected our fire's bright blaze.

I wondered wherever he'd find,
  In that very rough wintry weather,
A shelter away from the wind,
  That now and then ruffled a feather.

I invited him in, if he 'd come,
  To have shelter and supper with me ;
And he deigned but to pick up a crumb,
  And then he preferred liberty.

To be free on the poor leafless brier,
  He thought was a far safer plan,
Than to trust for a supper and fire,
  The capricious dominion of man.

THE BIRD-CATCHER.

A linnet was singing in Riv'lin
  As it flitted from bramble to thistle;
And I heard, in the fresh morning air,
  Both it and a robinet whistle.

As happy as songsters in heaven,
  Their warblings were liquidly tender,
As the haze of the morn cleared away,
  And the sun came out in his splendour.

That morning a bird-catcher came,
  And he bird-limed the twigs of a sloe,
And his cagèd decoy-bird he placed
  On a fragment of sandstone below.

I persistently loitered about,
  To warn the poor victims away
From the snare he had set for them there;
  And I cared not for what he'd to say.

A low-lived bird-cagey smell
  From the rags of his body arose,
And all that he was was repulsive,
  His looks, his abuse, and his clothes.

I felt nearly as sorry for him,
    As I did for the victims he 'd got;
For the clutches of brutality
    Had hopelessly seized on his lot.

When the days of sad bondage are o'er,
    And his soul and his birds are set free;
They 'll forgive him and whistle in Paradise,
    I hope both for him and for me.

THE HEDGEHOG.

Dusky, dark, speckled, and spiny,
  As sharp as the whin bush's thorn ;
Not a moment but on the defensive,
  Nocturnal and hedge-bottom born.

Persistently rolled in a ball,
  He 's had many a siege to sustain
Of dog, fox, pole-cat, and viper,
  That life might longer remain.

And then he has hunted his prey,
  And dabbled his muzzle with blood,
And after slived back to his hole,
  To nourish a famishing brood.

Tho' guarded with instinct and prickles,
  Life's terms with him are severe,
For his principal effort 's defence,
  And little is left for life's cheer.

If he 'd yield but to civil restraint,
  He should have food, protection and ease,
But it seems he would rather be wild,
  And trust to his Maker for these.

THE KITTEN.

Eh ! gamboling poor little kitten,
   How hard thou hast struggled to live ;
For burnt, scalded, lost, and dog-bitten,
   Thy life has gone thro' the small sieve.

A month or two back and we 'd got,
   Both thee and a pert little brother ;
But now we know not his lot,
   And besides we 've lost the old mother.

How fleeting thy sorrows must be,
   For the day they are come, they are gone
And again thou playest in glee
   With my lace, as my shoes I put on.

One day and thy troubles are o'er,
   Nor pains on the morrow incroach ;
And again thou art happy once more,
   For thou hast not thyself to reproach.

Like thine my griefs would be less
   If myself I had not to blame,
But this alas ! I confess
   Thy trials and mine are n't the same.

If always we did best we could,
   How few our sorrows would be ;
And they I believe never would
   Descend to real misery.

MY OWN BELOVED BOY.

———

I.

My own beloved boy, as if
  Thou wert mine eye, I see
All things thro' thee, and gladness smiles
  Wherever thou mayest be.

No light can light the heart like love;
  Or daisies in the grass
Would be no dearer things to us
  Than buttons made of brass.

Boyhood was sweet to me in Rivelin—
  My days were purer then,
And happy recollections left
  Behind are dear to men,

Who having mingled with a world
  Of hateful, spurious things,
Would change its vanities at last
  For peace which pure life brings.

II.

I wore a spencer then,
  And rosettes on each string
That tied my hat, when first
  I heard a cuckoo sing

In Rivelin, when the month
  Was May time, and the air
In balmy zephyrs moved
  The new-leaved branches, where

The finch and willow-wren
  Sang carelessly and sweet,
As tho' cold winter's face,
  They never more should meet.

III.

My father took me there ;
  For he his boyhood spent
In Rivelin valley, and
  Instinctively we went

There, soon as I could walk,
  Our leisure to enjoy ;
As I go now with thee,
  My own belovèd boy !

IV.

These hills, creation's size,
　Surround thee, and impress
Thy finer feelings with
　Their breadth and mightiness;

In their repose, they stoop
　Not to be merely great,
Nor beautiful—serene
　Sublimity's their state.

These rustic homes of man,
　Mid half-wild steepy fields,
Where rough land tardily
　To cultivation yields,

Bring into feeling life,
　The first emotions of
The heart that vibrates with
　The tender pulse of love.

V.

'T is heart the world needs most—
　'T were better be insane,
Than be without a heart
　To civilize the brain:

And should to men this high
   Intelligence be given,
Men would be better then,
   And earth more like to heaven.

VI.

My dear boy's ignorance
   Remove, O God! that he
May know Thy ways: awake
   His sensibility,

That sinfulness may be
   Too hateful to endure,
That chaste may be his thoughts,
   And all his pleasures pure.

THE BANKS OF THE BLACK BROOK; OR, ELLIOTT'S "RIBBLEDIN."

TO A DEAD LEAF TINGED WITH HOAR FROST.

Thou little frosty leaf
  Where many a grassy blade
Is like a silver spear
  Embroidered thou art laid.
And where the narrow shadow
  Of many a grassy stem
Is thrown athwart thy bosom
  Thou art a peerless gem.

The silvery lace is beautiful
  On every crimp and fold ;
But touching thee more nearly
  Thy vesture is but cold.
Thou art the likest Fancy
  Of ought where'er I stray,
For e'en before my breathing
  Thy spangles melt away.

Tho' to my flesh thou canst
  No earthly comfort bring,
In Fancy's sphere thy robe
  Would fit a fairy king.
In our accounts of goods
  We could not reckon thee,
Yet Fancy sets thee down
  In her inventory.

Thus Fancy sees in thee
  A worth to flesh unknown,
And gives thy hoary mantle
  A value of her own.

BETSY WAIT.

She knows not where to go ;
  No way of life seems left ;
Alone, undone, deceived,
  Of every hope bereft.

She never had a thought
  But to be his loyal wife ;
She never loved another,
  But him she loved as life.

The night is getting late ;
  The street is wet and cold ;
A strange man follows her,
  And plucks her garment's fold :

She knows not where to go—
  There seems no other fate,
But early death for her.
  Alas ! poor Betsy Wait.

O heartless selfishness
  That can wrest all away,
And care not what becomes
  Of poor despisèd clay.

It was not she was idle
  That this should be her fate,
For loving and hard working
  Was orphan Betsy Wait.

THE LOST LAD.

Faintly is seen a lone star in the West,
  The object of many an eye,
And between the black clouds, as they ride
    on the blast,
  It flits o'er the fields of blue sky.

The trees round the homestead are roaring
    and breaking,
  The old hollow chimneys are groaning,
The crazy worn doors on their hinges are
    squeaking,
  And the ghosts in the cocklofts are moan-
    ing.

Yet e'en beyond this, on the moors far
    away,
  Where the hailstones are rising, then
    ceasing,
Where the rills o'er the rocks in white
    snowy spray
  Are blown on the blast that is freezing.

Even there, where the road o'er the moor-
   lands so bare
  Is like to some river's meander,
The lost Irish lad in the pitiless air
  Unfed and half naked does wander.

He looks at the clouds as they sweep o'er
   the moss,
  And his heavenward eyes are in tears ;
His scarlet cold hand o'er his heart makes a
   cross,
  And his lips are quick muttering in prayers.

The long road before him is weary to dree,
  And his red face is beaten with wind
Too strong for his breath, and he turns round
   to see
  The miles and the darkness behind.

Then turning again with his face to the West,
  Where the twilight illumines the sky,
That star streams its light on the tears that
   have rest
  On the lids of his swimming blue eye.

But look! 'tis a shepherd he sees coming
   yonder,
  And when they shall meet he will say—
" From some warm human dwelling how far
   do I wander,
  Thus lost and alone on my way? "

" The Snake Inn is next," says the shepherd
    when met,
  As the wind scarce permits him to stay,
" But the Snake Inn my lad lies much further
    yet,"
  Then he winds o'er the moorlands away.

The lad is left gazing at hills in the West,
  Where lingers a remnant of day,
Where the shepherd's vague finger had
    pointed him rest,
  But he sees not where Snake Inn doth lay.

The blast hurries fast o'er the bent and the
    heather,
  On the mountains so wild and so steep,
Where alone with the lost Irish lad in the
    weather
  Are starved but a few scattered sheep.

He looks at the mountains around the bleak
    moss,
  And his strained aching eyes are in tears,
His scarlet cold hand o'er his heart makes a
    cross,
  And his lips are still muttering in prayers.

Long past is the shepherd, the gale blows
    still on,
  It carries a single snow flake,
The sky is still cloudy, more dreary 't has
    gone,
  And the shelterless moors are all bleak.

He looks for Snake Inn, and he looks for a
    light,
  But valleys before him are dimmer,
And all he can see in the bosom of night
  Are mountains that show not a glimmer.

Not a wall for a shelter along the highway,
  Not a shed, not a hut to be seen,
And the snowflakes in numbers began now
    to play,
  And the frosty cold blast to blow keen.

He looks at the darkening of night o'er the
    moss,
  And his heavenward eyes are in tears,
His scarlet cold hand o'er his breast makes
    a cross,
  And his lips are still muttering in prayers.

He's sickening at heart, he staggers, he lags,
  For his strength and his feelings are spent,
And the storm beating in at his loops and
    his rags,
  He lies down on a tussock of bent.

The night darkens yet, the storm rages still,
  It drives o'er the lost Irish lad;
He's laid in the white snow, he's pale, and
    he's chill,
  He's laid in the air and is dead.

The storm is subsiding, the clouds are
    dividing,
  And the stars are now rolling in space,
And the lost Irish lad in the snow is abiding,
  A dead beauty in heaven's blue face.

He still seems to gaze at the stars o'er the
    moss,
  His lips again never shall speak,
His hand's on the breast it so lately did
    cross,
  And his tears freezing fast on his cheek.

OLD RUTH.

The month of August
  Had just begun,
And sweltering was the glorious weather
  Beneath a burning sun.

Both man and beast
  Their toiling stayed,
And wearied with the Summer's heat
  They sought the cooling shade.

The trees were calm,
  The leaves were still,
All things were hushed in Summer silence,
  All but the bubbling rill,

Or save the buzzing
  Of the wild bees,
And ceaseless murmuring of Summer flies
  In swarms upon the trees,

When an old woman
  Of seventy years
Who 'd lived a long time by a wood,
  Where a lone cot appears,

Then left her home,
  And o'er the green
She went beneath the shady trees
  That by that path are seen.

A wide black bonnet
　　Was on her head,
Her comely gown was plain and slack,
　　Her wearing shawl was red.

She 'd in her hand
　　A small blue can ;
She went for water for her kettle,
　　Where some lone streamlet ran.

Upon a staff
　　She forward bent,
And 'tween the trees the sun shone on her,
　　As slowly by she went.

Beside the hedge
　　So thick and green,
Beneath the docks and hemlocks flowed
　　The tinkling stream unseen.

The old worn stones
　　Which there were laid
Amid the short smooth grass uneven
　　A crooked footpath made.

At length beside
　　A gate and stile
Where stones were laid no further, the good
　　Old woman stayed awhile.

Towards the gate
  She walked unsteady,
She raised her sunken eye and said
  " The corn is ripe and ready.

" This glorious weather
  Is hastening past
The reapers should ere long be at it ;
  'T is ripening very fast."

Then on the gate her
  Hand she raised,
And on the distant sunny hills
  With mazy sight she gazed.

Her feelings moved,
  She breathed a sigh,
And sweet reflection's tear had dimmed
  Her mazy sunken eye.

The power of memory
  So sweetly broke
Upon her soul and in the sunshine
  The good old woman spoke.

" Ah ! I see it again
  Yon small white cot
On yonder distant sunny hills,
  That is my native spot.

" The time has fled
    'T will never more
Return when I in youth lived there
    In happy days of yore."

She died what time
    She 'd been Ruth Street
Full eighty years ; and now her name
    Is getting obsolete.

EVENING IN JUNE.

THE FALL OF NIGHT.

The sun was just setting
　O'er hills in the West,
Where cloudlets were floating
　Like gold fish at rest.

Noah's Ark was then streaking
　The heavens so high,
And like a hay-raking
　It stretched o'er the sky,

When cattle were lowing
　As homeward they drew,
When daisies were bowing,
　And falling the dew.

The cuckoo was singing,
　And gurgling the rill;
The time-bell was ringing,
　And evening was still.

The trees were all deadening
　In stillness and hushed,
The heavens were reddening,
　The woodlands were flushed.

The insects were playing
   And commencing to bite,
The donkey was braying
   In the silence of night.

The brooms were all yellow,
   The field-fires were burning,
And from the dry fallow
   The swain was returning,

When to rest him he stayed,
   And he sat on a rail
Where his rake he had laid,
   And he looked on the vale

Where the trout were oft leaping ;
   And quickly the swallows
Were curving and sweeping
   For flies on the shallows.

The blackbird and throstle
   That cheered the green alley
Were ceasing to whistle
   As night owned the valley.

Straight up in the air
   The cottage was smoking,
And folk that were there
   He could hear they were talking.

Their bidding good night
  And the scream of the gate,
Of the spring in its flight
  He could hear as he sate.

On the village quoit-ground
  The quoits were still ringing,
And some boy homeward bound
  Was whistling and singing.

Some amateur playing
  His bugle was heard,
While darkness was laying
  Its robe on the sward.

The children together
  Were making a din,
And the cry of a mother
  Was calling them in.

From a long summer's roam
  The geese were returning,
They slowly came home,
  And the goslings were mourning.

What night-sounds they made
  While nestling they lay,
Which on the green glade
  Died slowly away.

As up he was rising
  To go for the night,
At the North he was gazing
  While still there was light.

As home he was straying
  At the North he would stare,
Repeatedly saying
  " No night will be there."

A MOONLIGHT FROSTY NIGHT.

The sky was clear,
  The moon was bright,
The frost was hoary on the fields
  One cold December night.

The rocky cliff,
  The mountain steep,
Were peering through the flimsy mist
  Among their sides asleep.

The moonlight hills,
  The keen frost white
And silvery, babbling wayside well
  Were beautiful that night.

When slowly came
  A black horse striding,
And in the clumsy cart he hurried ;
  Two farmers home were riding.

They came along
  The rugged way,
And when they crossed the ford, they saw
  The glittering water play.

Through leafless trees
  The moon was peeping,
As went the slow, old, rattling cart,
  When lawns and woods were sleeping.

Through naked twigs
  The moon was gliding,
And ever with them as they went,
  Still homeward slowly riding.

Beneath the wheels,
  Old, dry, and creaking,
As on the hard, white lane they went,
  The weak thin ice was breaking.

And when they passed
  That ruined place,
The Murrod farm, the horse yet kept
  His slow unaltered pace.

They saw those black,
  Old walls that night,
And ruined windows, where the moon
  Displayed her silvery light.

At length they reached
  The Fullod well,
At which the old horse stayed to drink,
  And the heavy cart was still.

They slacked the rein,
 They heard him drinking,
And silence settled on their ears,
 When not a chain was clinking.

But now the old
 Horse raised his head,
With water rattling from his mouth,
 And stirred with heavy tread.

THE SOLITARY FIR TREE.

I.

One Summer day
  Beneath a cloudless sky
I had wandered
  A weary and long way,
Where'er the road meandered,
  Which was hot and dry,
Which o'er the moors did stray.

The moors were brown and wide
  Till they were bound
With hazy blue sky,
  And there was nothing beside
To relieve the ear or sight
  Unless it was the flight
Of distant birds, or the startling cry
  Of grouse, which was the only sound
That broke the monotony around.

Thus loitering alone
  Beneath a burning sun
I began to be weary.
  The buzzing bees,
On the flowering heath,
  And the running lizards beneath
No more could please;
  And every thing was dreary.

Slowly onward I went
  Void of thought,
And caring for nought,
  Till another mile was spent ;
And then I saw in the West,
  On the brow of a little hill,
A lonely stone fir tree,
  Whose top seemed to be
A small Summer cloud at rest,
  Remaining quite still,
Or like that that was like a man's hand
That Elijah saw in Mount Carmel's land.

The tree was alone,
  And at its foot was laid
A mighty stone,
  Where many a stroller had stayed,
And the bole of the tree
  I could but faintly see,
For what came to my eye
  Was its top in the sky.

As it seemed to be a resting place,
  I quickened my pace,
Hoping to find
  On the brow of the hill
A faint breathing of pleasant wind,
  For the day was hot and still.

Weary and overheated,
  At length I was seated

On that mighty block of stone,
  Which with lichens had gone
Green and gray,
  Ere ever I had been that way.

Initials and dates were seen
  Upon it everywhere,
Some had been
  Cut two hundred years past,
And others but lately, the last
  Of which bore the date of the passing
        year.

And where the rain falls
  Upon that mighty block,
Were hollowed holes
  That a little water bore,
Which remained
  Since the last time it rained,
When the storm passed o'er
  That lonely rock.

On the lowest end
  Of that curious stone
I sat alone,
  Willing to spend
Some time in rest;
  For wearisome was the way,
And I was much oppressed
  With the heat
Of that Summer day.

The afternoon was flying
　　While there I stayed,
And was backward laid
　　Listening to the sighing
Of that solitary
　　Stone fir tree.

For ever and for ever
　　In a ceaseless monotony,
Like some languishing lover
　　It sighed mournfully.

In Fancy's ear
　　It sounded to be
The flying pages
　　Of time, year after year,
Rustling hastily
　　To departed ages
For ever turning to the past.

II.

To lie down on the ground,
　　On the summit of a hill,
In the zephyrus summer time,
　　Where a pine tree murmurs still,

You can feel as if earth moved:
　　And to that tree's tone, but hark,
And you fancy that you hear
　　They are burning Joan of Arc.

For the hum of ages gone
 Seem to linger in that tree ;
And the moving mass of Israel
 Leaves a tone behind to me.

And those storm-bent branches show,
 By their leaning all one way,
What the Western winds have done—
 But they are at peace to-day,

Lulled with dream-love that I feel
 When Æolus plays an air
On his wild harp, and a child's
 Waxy fingers comb my hair,

Or that when I am at church
 On a Summer Sunday morn,
When the June rose scent is sweet,
 On the wings of Zephyrus borne.

For he comes to church in Summer
 To hear Urania sing,
Comes in thro' open windows
 On his hayfield scented wing.

And he fans the parson's brow,
 As if with the leaves of palms ;
And the labourer joins as well
 In the singing of the Psalms.

And the heavenly Litany
 Comes from his emotional breast
Whose rough hand soils his prayer
 Book leaves on the day of rest.

THE WITCH.

I.

No moon was shining that night,
  And midnight sleepers were dreaming,
When snow-buried fields were all white,
  And the Northern lights were streaming.

O'er hills all covered with snow,
  The stars in heaven were beaming;
When all was then night-time below,
  And the Northern lights were streaming.

The North-wind blew and was dreary;
  The forest-trees desolate seeming,
When the damn'd of their torments were
      weary,
  And the Northern lights were streaming.

Jin Swinkill stood on a cliff,
  The hoarse night-raven was screaming,
When her limbs were aged, crazy, and stiff,
  And the Northern lights were streaming.

She gazed at Orion in heaven,
  Whose fiery armour was gleaming;
And the stars in Pleiades were seven,
  And the Northern lights were streaming.

She ne'er could cast a nativity—
  Her weird was nothing but seeming,
A vile semi-barbarous proclivity,
  When the Northern lights were streaming.

II.

She never remembered her mother,
　Who died when she was a child,
Leaving five in this wilderness-world
　With a father abandoned and wild.

Ill usage had broken her spirit,
　And little she said when she died,
Not e'en to her baby that played
　With flowrets they brought to her side.

Their father neglected their home,
　And seldom at night he was there;
Till the wolves of starvation and vice,
　Leapt the threshold and made it their lair.

The friendship of neighbours fell off;
　And the last ties began to decay;
So they started to prowl out at night,
　And seldom were seen in the day.

They all of them came to bad ends;
　And she had oft slept in a ditch;
And ne'er knowing what kindness could be,
　She naturally turned to a Witch.

She ne'er put her foot on the nicks
　Of the pavement; and never passed paling
Without superstitiously touching
　And carefully counting each railing.

How strange are the mind's phenomena,
   Its selfishness, frenzy, and fears !
The strong cruel hearted with lust,
   And the weak damping earth with their
     tears.

The fanatical raving to idols
   Of spirit, of stone, or of wood ;
And the wicked viciously craving
   For gold, silk, wine, and blood.

Whose heart is n't touched when he hears
   The wild wail of human distress,
Arising from ignorant fears,
   Strong passions and helplessness ?

God speed thee, Philanthropy,
   Thy heart is great and refined,
Exploring the dreary regions
   Of the rude and uninformed mind.

THE QUARRYMAN.

He's pulling down a hill,
With crowbar, pick, and drill,
And shots like muffled thunder—
He's rending earth asunder.
And with his heavy sledge,
He smites the iron wedge ;
And splits up into blocks,
The massivest of rocks.

In solitudes of stone,
He labours on alone ;
And like a quarry elf,
He's the colour of his delf :
And every weary blow
Re-echos to and fro ;
Stone getting from that den,
To build the homes of men.

For forty years and more,
As his father did before,
He's laboured in that gap,
In very nature's lap.

And if there 's any shame,
Earth has herself to blame ;
For ere he e'er wore shoe,
She might know what he 'd do.

She 'll let him have his way,
His life time to a day,
And bear no malice then ;
And with the rest of men,
He 'll have a burial place—
And the beetle's hurried pace
Shall cross his gravestone letters,
Nor heeding him nor his betters.

RIVELIN'S WATERS, SONG, AND SUNRISE.

I.

Dear Rivelin vale,
With all my senses charmed,
   I pace thy dewy lawns ;
And sip at crystal springs,
   That bathe thy mossy stones.

Thy limpid rills,
O'er sandstone rocks, their long
   White falling streams display,
As tulle adorns the bride,
   Upon her bridal day.

Thy peat-stained brooks,
That leap from heathery hills,
   In skyey lustre flow ;
And look like strings of pearls
   On Egypt's swarthy brow.

Thy trickling springs,
Resplendent drops, do out
   Of gritstone measures leak ;
And bathe thy fragment rocks,
   As tears bathe Beauty's cheek.

Thy weightier streams
The slimy water wheel
　　Propel; and as it turns,
They fall like silken flounces
　　Among the fronds of ferns,

O'er Millstone Grit's
Day-peeping, basset edge,
　　Thy soft-toned waters run,
From fountains in the West,
　　Towards the morning sun.

II.

A matin song,
Thro' all the land salutes
　　This May-bright morn of Spring;
For myriads of birds,
　　At Rivelin's sunrise sing.

E'en Zephyrus stands,
With 'bated breath, to hear
　　The omnipresent tone;
As if like Memnon, hills
　　And valleys sang at dawn.

III.

Aurora's steeds
Come o'er the Eastern hills,
　　Pursuing shades of night,
That leave the dewy groves,
　　And take their Western flight.

Hail, charioteer!
Thou glorious One! to whom
   All eyes are turned this hour,
From every warbling bird,
   And every opening flower.

Apollo comes,
And on his lute he plays
   His lyrics sweet and tender;
And rays these rugged cliffs,
   With wild poetic splendour.

THE DANDELION.

Don't pull it up—
'T is a flower.
Well, but 't is a weed,
And it will run to seed.
Never mind, if it does—
It won't harm us—
Let it stop.
In the sunny hour,
It is one of Spring's
Prettiest things ;
And after the wintry glooms,
It is one of the flowers,
That are brought by April showers ;
And the sunniest and brightest that blooms.

EARLY POEMS

AND

LOVE SONGS.

MY NATIVE RIVELIN.

(The first Verses I ever wrote.)

It is thy stream so fair I see
The highest source of joy to me—
It fills my heart to think of thee,
                My native Rivelin.

I hear the lambs' unceasing bleather
Joyful in the Summer weather,
Playful on thy cliffs of heather,
                My native Rivelin.

Beneath thy beech and birken shade
The wearied heifer 's resting laid,
Contented on the grassy glade.
                My native Rivelin.

The high noon sun unclouded burns
And labouring men have left their " turns "
Till cooler are thy solstial urns,
                My native Rivelin.

The quickens droop before the blaze,
The yellow flowers steadfast gaze
Despite the force of solar rays,
                My native Rivelin.

The fly 's the only lively thing
That steadies on its gauzy wing,
And now and then that takes a fling,
    My native Rivelin.

The throstle keeps a shady seat,
Among the hawthorn blossoms sweet,
To pass the noon of Summer heat,
    My native Rivelin.

Thy silver streams their pride abate,
And country boys together prate
Paddling in thy half-dried gait,
    My native Rivelin.

But venting here my bosom's swell
Thy flying hour forbids me dwell,
And I must part with thee—Farewell!
    My native Rivelin.

ON PRESENTING A WILD ROSE TO MY FIRST SWEETHEART.

(One of my earliest attempts at Verse.)

———

At Nature's hand, in wild display
　　The rose spontaneous grew,
Whose simple virtues love convey
　　No Art can e'er imbue.

Then may it die but with reward—
　　Not languish in despair ;
Such is thy lover's true regard,
　　His only wish and prayer.

SONG.

———

Thou gurgling Porter, hush thy sound,
　　Thy streams are nought to me;
The weeping birch in groups around
　　Alone give sympathy.
Forbear to sing, thou little wren,
　　That warbles o'er the stream,
And on the glade, thou setting sun
　　Withhold thy golden beam.

Withhold, bright Heavens, all your charms,
　　This calm, this Summer eve,
Or fold my Martha in these arms,
　　And this sad heart relieve.
But ah! upon this downy grass,
　　She walks not by my side:
My falling tears my grief confess—
　　She ne'er may be my bride.

BOB WINNMOOR.

I'm sure I've seen that face;
But I do n't remember where.
'T was quite a stare
    Came from that eye,
    As he passed by,
At a church-yard pace.
It cannot be amiss,
To turn back and ask who it is.
    Why! it's Bob Winnmoor—
I have n't seen him for years;
But how weakly and ill he appears—
    I doubt he's poor.

I'll not merely doubt it,
But I'll know more about it.
Poor Bob! he was n't a fool,
I knew him and liked him and boxt with
    him when we went to school.

CRICKET.

On the bright sunny field,
 We 'll pitch the light wicket ;
 In the turf we will stick it,
 Where 't is levelled for cricket,
On the bright sunny field.

On the bright sunny field,
 The bowler assails
 The three stumps and the bails ;
 And he often prevails
On the bright sunny field.

.On the bright sunny field,·
 They fall at his hands,
 Till some batter withstands
 All the skill he commands,
On the bright sunny field.

On the bright sunny field,
 Be cheerful and fair ;
 For calm courage and care
 Will win the match there,
On the bright sunny field.

On the bright sunny field,
 Keep adding one more
 Even to a small score ;
 'T is not lost till 't is o'er
On the bright sunny field.

THE LION.

I.

Appalling monster, thy bones are broad
  And powerfully made ;
But stronger still the massy load
  Of muscles on them laid.

Thy heavy and elastic skin
  Is plentifully thrown
O'er thy loose limbs : thy mane is in
  Dark tangled masses grown.

Thine eye, like Cæsar's, sees the crowd,
  But deigns to look on no
One in particular ; but proud
  And calm, turns to and fro.

The strength those iron bars must be,
  With not a guard neglected,
Show even in captivity,
  That thou must be respected,

And every care be taken, lest
   Thou should'st arise and smite
Them by.   I think I see thee prest
   With that great appetite,

Which would lay man convulsed in dust,
   Were he to feel it but
A moment; or that terrible lust,
   Thou hast when thou would'st glut

Thy raging maw with bloody fill
   Warm from thy victim's vein;
Beneath tempestuous growls, that still
   Burst from thee o'er the slain.

And yet magnanimous art thou;
   For having few to fear,
Repose is mostly on thy brow,
   And panic seldom there.

II.

There is a universal AM,
   That has no negative,
That gives existence to the lamb,
   And makes the lion live.

As clay fits to the potter's mould,
   They grow to laws that bind them,
And all the strange forms we behold
   Must e'en be as we find them.

They are the children of years,
   That work out types with ease ;
And in dentition there appears
   Some crude account of these.

THE HYENA.

Unweariedly pacing about,
  From the back of thy den to the rails,
As tho' thou would'st wear a way out,
  With the scratling tips of thy nails.

But surely thou art hopeless of this,
  And 't is only to wear away hours,
Or some keeper may yet be remiss,
  Forgetting thy vigilant powers.

It is nature, not hope, that compels
  Thee to search for release—on the failings
Of men keen watchfulness tells,
  And corrosion may weaken the railings.

They say thou art nearly too savage
  To suckle the young of thy body,
That they often fall to the ravage
  Of thy hunger, rapacious and bloody.

Poor wretch ! thou art tortured with passions
   Thou hast not the power to subdue ;
Just breeding and breathing for rations,
   That are filthy, precarious, and few.

Then what is life's meaning to thee,
   If thou hast not before thee a goal ?
But a creature that merely must be,
   A link in a system—that's all.

TO LIZZIE.

O sweet beneath eve's golden wing
   When we walk twined together,
When mowers cease the scythe to swing,
   And leave the swath to wither.

And when the rose upon its brier
   Shuts up its lovely bloom,
And when the distant village spire
   Fades in the evening gloom.

All these with tender care I love,
   The rose, the ruddy West,—
But more than all, thy virtues move
   The feelings of my breast.

ELLEN.

The breeze on the meadow all waving is
    borne,
  As it flits from the West o'er the lea,
And moving so gently o'er rustling young
    corn
  It whispers reflections to me.

My sighs are unheard, and my bosom is torn,
  As I gaze with tears on yon dwellin',
For no more in my arms beneath the haw-
    thorn
  Shall be its fair inmate, my Ellen.

The sky that unites with the landscape is
    clear,
  And blossoms adorning the furrow,
Like vessels of crystal to view they are fair,
  But for me are containing but sorrow.

O, why should fond Nature such beauty have
    lent
  For Fortune to mock with a tear?
Or why with misfortune my feelings have
    blent,
  And still have allowed me to see her?

But yet may the sorrow now breaking my
    heart
  Ne'er canker her bosom so fair,
For tho' she has certainly bid me depart,
  'T is love she has doomed to despair.

FAR FROM THEE.

Thy Harry, Ellen, far from thee
  Where birch and hazels grow ;
Thy Harry, Ellen, far from thee
  Where Rivelin's waters flow,
Thy Harry, Ellen, far from thee
  Shall tune the lyre again,
But Harry, Ellen, far from thee
  Shall tune the lyre in vain.

These streams, that white as silver rill
  Their rocky slabs among,
These streams that once my heart could fill
  O'erflowing with a song ;
These streams no more my bosom thrill
  Nor ever sound so clear,
And though these streams be native still
  My love shall languish here.

EMMA.

The linnet 's happy in its bush,
   The cuckoo on the tree,
The wren beneath some mossy roof,
   And I am blest with thee.

I care not what 's beyond yon hills,
   Nor heed what 's doing there,
So long as thou, my soul's desire,
   Art loitering with me here.

What though the grass beneath our feet
   Is e'en not mine to give thee,
I yet do give a lover's heart,
   That never can deceive thee.

The heart 's the seat of happiness,
   It is the throne of love ;
And if we have but loving hearts,
   We 're blest where'er we rove.

MARY.

My Mary stole my boyish heart
   When we were making hay;
My Mary stole my boyish heart,
   And won my soul away.

We raked the hay in heaps together,
   Our converse sweetly wandered,
I felt the tide enraptured flow
   That through my frame meandered.

I could no longer rake in heaps
   The fragrant hay so sweet,
And by her in the last we 'd made
   I found a happy seat.

I whispered that she 'd stolen my heart;
   Her breast beat at my side,
And trifling with a stem of hay,
   She reddened and she sighed.

She let me clasp her in my arms,
   I felt her burning cheek;
I asked her if she would be mine,
   But Mary could not speak.

I felt her boiling tears o'erflow,
   I felt her beating heart,
I prest her to my aching breast,
   And wished we ne'er could part.

Some silent moments thus ensued,
   And peace at length returned;
Her heaving heart was beating less,
   Her cheek less hotly burned.

My arms less tightly clasped her waist,
   Yet how unplighted sever?
Again I asked her to be mine,
   And whispered she—" For ever."

MARTHA.

I must leave thee, my Martha, I must leave
thee, 't must be ;
  I must leave thee, but leave thee with
  sorrow and pain ;
For that cruel decree, which now parts me
from thee,
  May never permit me to see thee again.

When alone on my own native hills I shall
wander,
  And look at the dark rising cliffs of the
  North,
As the clouds shall pass o'er them my heart
shall grow fonder,
  And my eyes shall still gaze the way of
  thy birth.

And when a snow shower shall wet the
March blossom,
  And a snow flake shall fall, bedimming my
  sight,
Let me think it 's a kind thought direct from
thy bosom,—
  Thy bosom as lovely, as spotless, as white.

JINNY.

Dost thou remember,
    When first that we met,
In the time of the roses,
    Which I ne'er can forget,
Tho' I see thee no more.

Dost thou remember
    How often we kist;
I think of those lips,
    Which so fondly I prest,
Tho' I see thee no more.

Dost thou remember,
    We plighted our love;
My idol of memory,
    Which I ne'er can remove,
Tho' I see thee no more.

Dost thou remember,
    The wild brier tree,
Whene'er I pass there,
    My thoughts are of thee,
Tho' I see thee no more.